Jamal's Journey

Michael Foreman

Andersen Press

This Book Belongs to

_____

For Louise

Author's note

When you are in Dubai, among its glistening glass towers, it is easy to forget
that this city was built in a desert and its roots are firmly in the Bedouin culture.
Central to that culture of course is the camel - the ship of the desert - who
provides so many things from transportation to racing and even milk chocolate.
During our visit to the Dubai Book Fair, my wife Louise fell in love with the camels
and when I discovered the word for beauty in Arabic is *jamaal*, the root
of which means 'camel', a story began to form in my mind.

This paperback edition first published in 2018 by Andersen Press Ltd.
First published in Great Britain in 2017 by Andersen Press Ltd.,
20 Vauxhall Bridge Road, London SW1V 2SA.
Copyright © Michael Foreman, 2017.
The rights of Michael Foreman to be identified as the author and
illustrator of this work have been asserted by him in accordance
with the Copyright, Designs and Patents Act, 1988.
All rights reserved.
Colour separated in Switzerland by Photolitho AG, Zürich.
Printed and bound in China.

1   3   5   7   9   10   8   6   4   2

British Library Cataloguing in Publication Data available.
ISBN 978 1 78344 591 2

Walk, walk, walk. That's what camels do.

It's all right for Jamal's mama and baba, they've got long legs.
He has little legs, so it's hard for him to keep up.
The people have little legs too, especially the boy,
but most of the time they don't walk. They ride.

Jamal looks at the falcons. They are lucky –
the birds get carried everywhere, except when they soar
through the sky, hunting the small creatures of the desert.
But Jamal is a little camel, and camels have to walk, walk, walk.

Suddenly there is a roaring noise.

Jamal doesn't know what is happening, there is sand everywhere,

whooshing and whirling in the wild wind!

Sand in his eyes. Sand in his nose. Sand in his ears.

"Mama! Baba!"
cries Jamal.

Now there is sand
in his mouth.

He turns his back to the howling wind,
making himself as small as possible.

The wind roars louder and louder,
thundering around him.
Then it stops as suddenly as it started.
The sand-filled sky has transformed
into a sky of stars.

"Mama! Baba!
Where are you?"

Jamal looks for footprints by the light of the moon,
but everything has been blown away by the wind.
Which way to go? With no clues,
Jamal just follows the moonlight.

Finally dawn breaks across the empty land of sand.

But it is not quite empty –
a tiny head with twitching
ears is looking at Jamal.

It is a jerboa!

Now a spiky monitor lizard peeps out from under a rock and a big brown hare bounces over the hill.

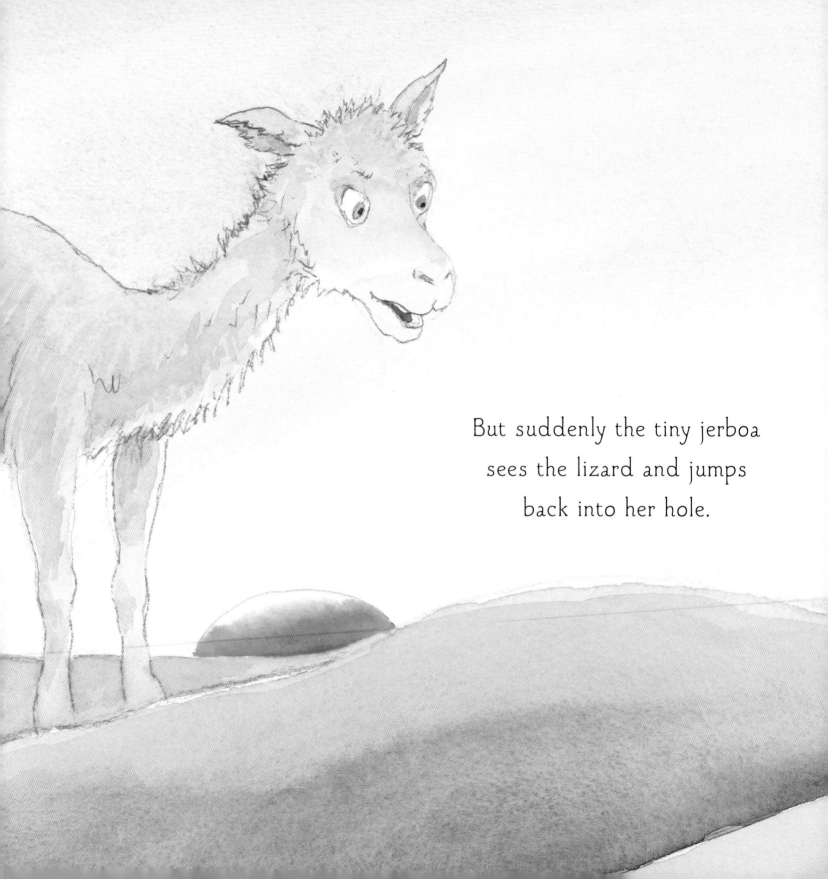

"Hello!" cries Jamal to them all.
"I am lost – can you help me?"

But suddenly the tiny jerboa
sees the lizard and jumps
back into her hole.

Then the lizard feels the vibrations as the big brown hare
hops closer and dives back under his rock.

A moment later the big brown hare twitches his huge ears,
looks up at the sky and races away, leaving Jamal alone again.

The lizard frightened the jerboa.
The hare frightened the lizard.
But what frightened the hare?

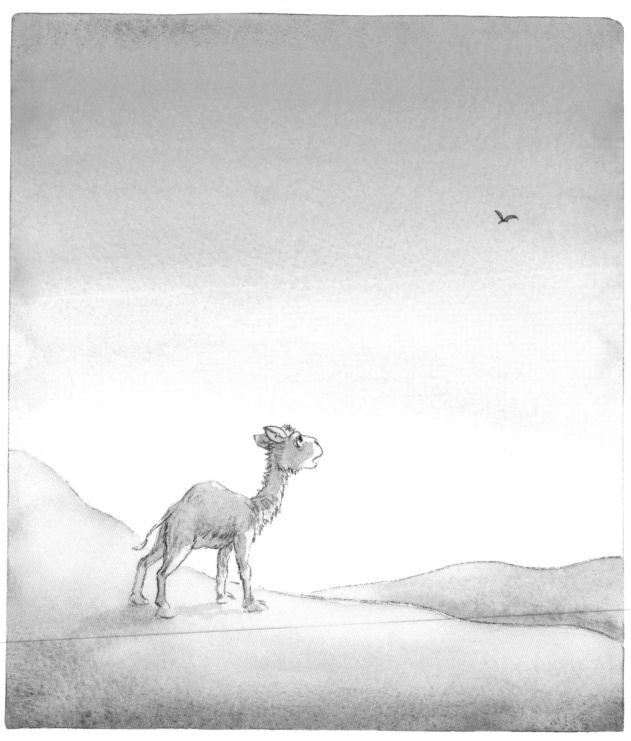

Jamal looks up to the sky and spots a tiny dot,
high in the blue, spiralling towards him.

It's a falcon, like the ones
who ride on Mama and Baba.

She hovers in front of Jamal
and then flies in a big loop.

As the little camel walks towards the falcon, she flies
a little further away and loops and loops again.
Jamal smiles. "This is fun!"

Jamal follows the falcon as it circles through the sky towards distant dunes. It's hot work climbing hills with his little legs.

"Oh!" cries Jamal. "I can see a great city, far away, and beyond that the shining sea!"

The falcon zooms off towards a cloud of dust that is moving slowly across the sandy plain and Jamal gallops after her.

In a short time she is whirling and looping in the air
with the other falcons. And the dust cloud has
turned and is coming back towards Jamal.

"Mama! Baba!" Jamal cries. But ahead of them all is
the boy – he is racing across the sand to hug his friend.

Together they all set off toward the faraway
city. Jamal stays close to Mama and Baba,
and the boy walks beside him: he doesn't
want his camel to get lost ever again.

Jamal had never been in a city before. It is so busy, so
noisy – the market, the boats, the sea. So exciting!

Now Jamal knows the world is more than just sand.
When his legs are long and strong, he wants to see it all.

One day, the boy will ride on him and Jamal
will walk, walk, walk, far and wide, from
gleaming cities to shining seas.

And he will always take his friendly falcon
along, just in case they get lost.